The Wild Bunch

Dee Lillegard

illustrated by
Rex Barron

G. P. Putnam's Sons   New York

To Camellia and Marielle . . . who helped—D.L.

*For my Phi Beta Kappa parents, who encouraged
both imagination and self-discipline—R.B.*

Library of Congress Cataloging-in-publication Data. Lillegard, Dee. The wild bunch/written by Dee Lillegard; illustrated by
Rex Barron. p. cm. Summary: Short verses provide light-hearted looks at all kinds of fruits and vegtables. 1. Children's poetry, American. 2. Fruit—Juvenile poetry. 3. Vegetables—Juvenile poetry. [1. Food—Poetry. 2. American poetry.] I. Barron,
Rex, ill. II. Title. PS3562.I4557W55 1997 811'.54—dc21 96-37483 CIP AC ISBN 0-399-22826-8
10 9 8 7 6 5 4 3 2 1   First Impression

ROOTS

Carrots, Turnips,
Radishes—Roots—
come from the ground
in dirty suits
and have to wash
for supper, too—
same as me,
same as you.

THE CARROT CLAN

The Carrots stick together
when they're in a crunch.
They pile up all their problems—
and solve them in a bunch.

GRANNY CAULIFLOWER

Granny gardened
with shovel and hoe—
Though the sun made her hot,
her head looked like snow.

**GREEN
BEAN
TEEN**

He's
tall
and
thin
and snappy
!
just
like
his
pappy
!
!

BUD BROCCOLI

Dark and handsome,
struts his stuff.
Flattery? Frankly,
he can't get enough!

GOOD KING PINEAPPLE

Looks forbidding,
but he's *sweet* . . .
no kidding.

JOE COCONUT

Hardheaded guy—
won't wear a tie.

ONION JOHN

Onion John, an appealing guy,
teased the Chives and made them cry.
When the Leeks came out to play,
Onion Johnny rolled away.

JONATHAN APPLE

Apples, Apples
of every variety—
the saucy sort
and Pie Society—
voted Jonathan
Pick of the Year,
which signaled the start
of his juicy career.

MUM'S THE FUNGUS

Mushrooms in their caps
are shy.
Speak to them—
they won't reply.

NEVER CALL AN EGGPLANT CHICKEN

They get purple in the face
and their heartbeats quicken—
if someone says, *Go lay an egg!*
or dares to call them
      Chicken.

THE GREAT ESCAPES
OF GREGORY GRAPES

Nothing could hold him.
He got loose
by squishing
himself
in-
to
j
u
i
c
e
.

PEACH AND NECTARINE

Peach and Nectarine—
you never saw the like.
One on her motorcycle,
one on her bike—
They both go riding
till they're pink in the cheeks.
Peach and Nectarine—
Nectarine and Peach.

LONG JOHN BANANA

A pirate with a tough exterior—
but soft inside—
with taste *superior*.

BING CHERRY

Bing Cherry sat upon a stone
and cried, *"Why am I all alone?*
Bighearted me, so sweet and fair . . .
Is it because I have no hair?"

THE MANGO

Rich and classy,
sometimes sassy.
Want to tango?
Ask the Mango.

BIG OLD PAPA PAPAYA

Big old Papa Papaya
wants breakfast rolls in bed—
but big old *Mama* Papaya
rolls Papa out instead.

UNCLE WATERMELON

Lazy one—
lies in the sun,
gets big and fat—
and he's *proud* of that!

A PAIR OF PEARS

All day and night,
a pair of Pears
did nothing more
than sit in chairs
and champ and chomp
on sugar loops.
Now they're a pair
of *nincompoops*.

COLONEL CORN

Said Colonel Corn,
 as he scratched his ear,
"I'm getting hard of hearing,
 I fear.
Or did the weather forecaster say,
It's going to be a buttery day?"

FREDERIC GARLIC

All the young Tomatoes say,
*Whenever Garlic comes to play,
he totally takes our breath*

                                away. . . ."

BELLE PEPPER

Charming Belle Pepper
was belle of the ball
till she ate—and got stuffed—
then sat wrapped in her shawl.

THE POTATO
VERSUS THE PEA

One potato
makes a meal.
One pea . . .
no big deal.

OKRA

Okra took a tumbo—
fell into the gumbo,
and swam with shrimp—
all *jumbo!*

A CUCUMBER QUESTION

You may think a Cucumber fickle
for not wanting to be a pickle.
Some don't.
Some do.
Would you?

A SWELLHEADED CITRUS

Lemon," said Lime, "you're never on time."
Said Lemon, "Let's not be sour.
   I know I am late.
   But I'm well worth the wait.
A week or a day or an hour. . . ."

FLORENCE SPINACH

Florence Spinach
wore nothing but green.
In anything else,
she refused to be seen.
"Can you imagine,"
I once heard her say,
"a Spinach in orange—
or yellow—or gray?"

BEATRICE BEET

Beatrice Beet
got it into her head
that all her dresses
should be red.
She soaked and dyed them,
all sixteen—
then colored her hair
a daring *green*.

IT'S A FIG FIG FIG FIG WORLD!

Flying figs go for rides.
Laughing figs split their sides.
Figs in hats . . .
Figs in shoes . . .
Figs on the freeway!
Front-page news!

Says Phineas Figg,
*"This fig sensation
is merely a figment
of your imagination. . . ."*